Megalosaurus

Stegosaurus

Baryonyx

Styracosaurus

Tyrannosaurus rex

For Alice

First published 2015 by Nosy Crow Ltd
The Crow's Nest, 10a Lant Street
London SE1 1QR
www.nosycrow.com

ISBN 978 0 85763 382 8 (PB)

Nosy Crow and associated logos are trademark
and/or registered trademarks of Nosy Crow Ltd.

A CIP catalogue record for this book is available from the British Library.

Printed in China

3 5 7 9 8 6 4

DINOSAUR ROCKET!

Penny Dale

nosy crow

Dinosaur rocket waiting,
waiting on the launch pad.
On the launch pad,
having final checks.

Astronaut dinosaurs riding,
riding on the bus.
On the bus, to the giant rocket.

Brave dinosaurs climbing,
climbing into the rocket.
Into the rocket,
right at the top.

Nervous dinosaurs pressing buttons,
pressing buttons and waiting to start.
Waiting to start . . .

... the dinosaur **countdown!**
10 ... 9 ... 8 ... 7 ... 6 ... 5 ...
4 ... 3 ... 2 ... 1 ... and ...

. . . lift off!

Dinosaur rocket roaring, roaring and thundering into space. Into space, zooming faster and faster!

Zoom!

Onto the moon,
in their dinosaur buggies!

Brrrm!

Proud dinosaurs posing,
posing with their flag.

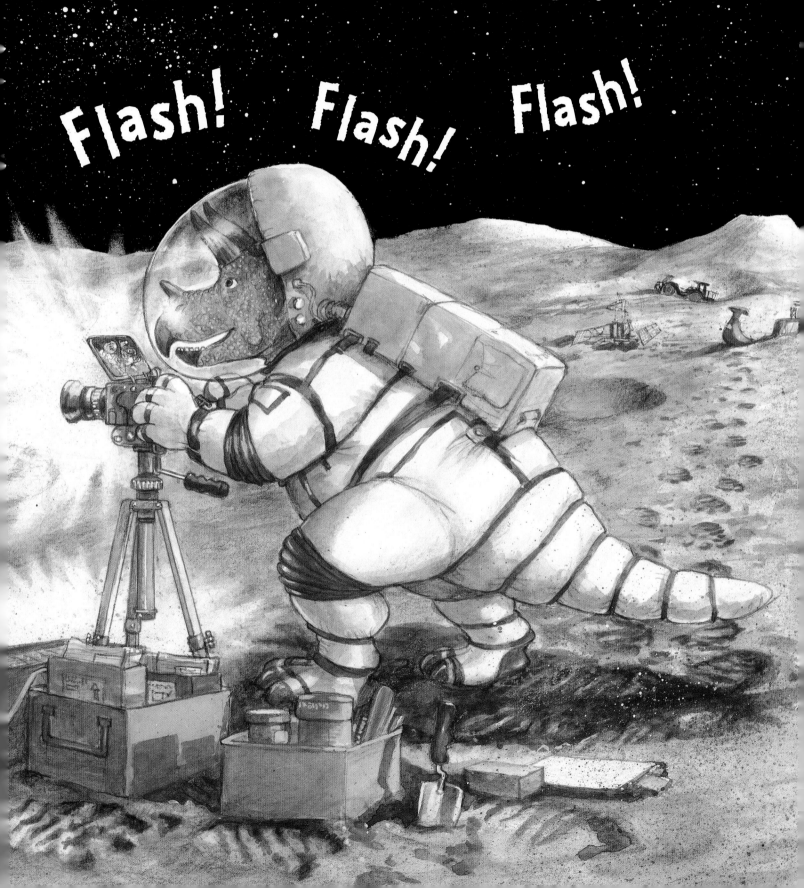

Laughing dinosaurs playing,
playing and floating in space!

Quiet dinosaurs stopping,
stopping to look at their planet.
Their blue planet, so far, far away...

Home!

Home!

Home!

Happy dinosaurs blasting off,
blasting off into space.
Into space, and on their way home.

Bye!

Hero dinosaurs splashing down,
splashing down, safe and sound.
Safe and sound, back on Earth!

Hurray!

Outside
Broadcast
Vehicle

RIB (Rigid Inflatable Boat)

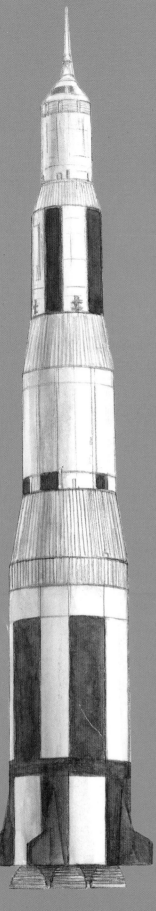

Moon
Buggy

Rocket

Pick-up Truck

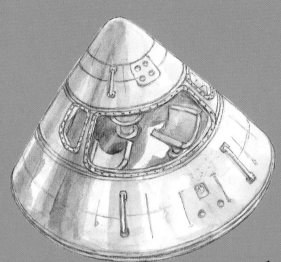

Landing Module

Astronaut Bus

Aircraft Carrier